Here's a story to share!

Sharing a story with your child is great fun and it's an ideal way to start your child reading.

The left-hand pages are 'your' story pages. The right-hand pages are specially written for your child with simple vocabulary and helpful repetition.

• Cuddle up close and look through the book together. What's happening in the pictures?

• Read the whole story to your child, both your story pages and your child's. Tell your child what it says on his* story pages and point to the words as you say them.

• Now it's time to read the story again and see if your child would like to join in and read his story pages along with you. Don't worry about perfect reading – what matters at this stage is having fun.

• It's best to stop when your child wants to. You can pick up the book at any time and enjoy sharing the story all over again.

Here the child is referred to as 'he'. All Ladybird books are equally suitable for both boys and girls.

Edited by Lorraine Horsley and Caroline Rashleigh
Designed by Alison Guthrie, Lara Stapleton and Graeme Hole
A catalogue record for this book is available from the British Library

Published by Ladybird Books Ltd
27 Wrights Lane London W8 5TZ
A Penguin Company

2 4 6 8 10 9 7 5 3 1

TEXT © TONY BRADMAN MCMXCVI
ILLUSTRATIONS © LADYBIRD BOOKS LTD MMI

This story was first published by Ladybird as What's Wrong with Bertie? MCMXCVI

LADYBIRD and the device of a Ladybird are trademarks of Ladybird Books Ltd

*All rights reserved. No part of this publication may be reproduced,
stored in a retrieval system, or transmitted in any form or by any means,
electronic, mechanical, photocopying, recording or otherwise,
without the prior consent of the copyright owner.*

Don't bother
Ben!

by Tony Bradman
illustrated by Rosalind Beardshaw

Ben was a very clever little bunny.
He could write the most amazing stories.
He could draw the most fantastic pictures.
And he could sing the most wonderful
songs. All Ben needed was some peace
and quiet.

But Ben the bunny had fourteen brothers
and sisters who always wanted to play with
him. "I like being on my own," Ben would
say, but they wouldn't listen.

Whenever he thought he was alone, along would come...

Boris and Betty and Billy and Belle, and Barry and Brenda and Brian as well, and Bobby and Bradley and Beattie and... yes, Barney and Beryl and Barbara and Bess. And they soon spoilt everything.

"Hey, Ben, can we play?" they would say, bouncing up and down. "Tell us a story! Draw us a picture! Sing us a song! Please, Ben. You're brilliant!"

"Oh, all right," Ben would say.

Ben loved his brothers and sisters, but he was fed up. He had to get some peace and quiet, or he would go bonkers! Then one day, Ben had an idea. He decided to try hiding from them.

Ben bided his time... then sneaked out of the bunny hole, and hoppity-hopped across the meadow as fast as he could go.

"They will never find me here," thought Ben, smiling to himself.

For a few delicious moments he was alone. It was very peaceful and quiet. Ben watched the frantic ants, he listened to the buzzy bees, and he sniffed the sweet-smelling flowers. But then along came...

Boris and Betty and Billy and Belle, and Barry and Brenda and Brian as well, and Bobby and Bradley and Beattie and... yes, Barney and Beryl and Barbara and Bess. And they soon spoilt everything.

"Hey, Ben!" they said, bouncing up and down. "What are you doing? Bet it's something really exciting. Can we play?"

"No, you can't," said Ben, crossly. Then he hoppity-hopped back to the bunny hole, muttering all the way.

That evening, Ben was a very grumpy bunny.

"What's wrong with Ben?" everybody wanted to know.

The next day, Ben decided to try hiding outside again.

Ben bided his time... then sneaked out of the bunny hole and hoppity-hopped to the bank of the river as fast as he could go.

"They will never find me here," he thought, smiling to himself.

13

For a few delicious moments he was alone.
It was very peaceful and quiet.
He watched the fish swishing, he listened
to the croaky frogs, and
he sniffed the rich muddy smell of
the river.

"I like being on my own!" thought Ben.

But then along came...

Boris and Betty and Billy and Belle, and
Barry and Brenda and Brian as well, and
Bobby and Bradley and Beattie and... yes,
Barney and Beryl and Barbara and Bess.
And they soon spoilt everything.

"Hey, Ben!" they said, bouncing up
and down. "There you are! For a while
we thought you were actually hiding
from us!"

"What gave you that idea?" said Ben,
crossly. Then he hoppity-hopped
back to the bunny hole,
muttering all the way.

There you are!

That evening, Ben was a very grumpy bunny indeed. In fact he was so grumpy, he even shouted... at his teddy bear!

"What's wrong with Ben?" everybody whispered.

The next day, Ben decided to try hiding outside one more time.

Ben bided his time... then sneaked out of the bunny hole and hoppity-hopped to the Wild and Windy Wood as fast as he could go.

"They will never find me here," he thought, smiling to himself.

He went in beneath the trees, where
it was very peaceful and very quiet.
He was truly, deliciously... alone at last.

Ben watched a seed pod twirling
and whirling down to the ground, he
listened to the birds twittering, he sniffed
the leaves, and felt the gentle evening
breeze.

"I like being on my own," he thought.

21

Ben thought of amazing new stories
to write, fantastic new pictures to
draw, and wonderful new songs to sing.
But there was something missing...
Ben had no one to share them with.
Besides, the sun was setting and the
darkness was creeping slowly towards
Ben. An owl hooted, and there was a
howling in the distance...

Suddenly, Ben heard a rustling in the
bushes. It got nearer and nearer and
nearer. Ben trembled with fear.

"Oh! I don't like being on my own!"
cried Ben.

Then along came...

Boris and Betty and Billy and Belle, and
Barry and Brenda and Brian as well, and
Bobby and Bradley and Beattie and... yes,
Barney and Beryl and Barbara and Bess.
They soon made Ben feel much better.

"Hey, Ben!" they said, bouncing up and
down. "There you are! Come on, there's a
surprise waiting for you at home!"

"A surprise? For me?" asked Ben,
puzzled.

Then fifteen brothers and sisters happily hoppity-hopped back to the bunny hole together, as fast as they could go.

That evening, Ben was a very... cheerful bunny. After all, he had no reason for gloom. Not now that he had his own little... room!

"I like having my own room," said Ben.

27

And who do you think were his very
first guests?

That's right!

Boris and Betty and Billy and Belle, and
Barry and Brenda and Brian as well, and
Bobby and Bradley and Beattie and... yes,
Barney and Beryl and Barbara and Bess.
And they all said...